CATUNDRA

Weekly Reader Books presents
CATUNDRA

Written By:
STEPHEN COSGROVE

Illustrated By:
ROBIN JAMES

A Serendipity Book

This book is a presentation of Weekly Reader Books.
Weekly Reader Books offers book clubs for children from
preschool through high school.

For further information write to:
Weekly Reader Books
4343 Equity Drive
Columbus, Ohio 43228

Dedicated to Catapuss, the cat that originally inspired this story, and Maxwell the cat, Uncle Mable, Pancake, Smokey, Skunk, Munch, Retard, Nicki, Angel, and all the other fat cats in the world.

Steve

In a perfect part of the forest, in a land of fur, purrs, and meows, stood an old dilapidated cabin that no one had lived in for a long, long time.

The cabin was in such poor shape that none of the creatures of the forest would live there. None, that is, except a rag tag, fat cat called Catundra. She lived there because it was the only place where she could hide from the other animals who would laugh and call her names. Catundra, you see, had always been just a little bit plump; you could, in fact, call her downright fat.

From dawn to dusk, whenever the other creatures of the forest would pass the old cabin, they would shout out and call her names: "Catundra is a fatty, Ninner-ninner-ninners!" or sometimes they'd jeer, "We'd better run away because fat Catundra might waddle over here and sit on us!" Then, after chanting their nasty remarks, they would run into the forest amidst gales of laughter.

Poor Catundra would feel so bad after their name-calling that she felt she just had to do something to forget what they had said and so she would eat more and more. Every time she ate some more she got just a little fatter, which made her feel worse and so she ate some more.

Every day it was the same thing over and over, until Catundra became so fat that she could barely walk at all.

Then, one day, it happened that she could find nothing to eat. She looked in her favorite spot for catching mice but they were all gone. She waddled over to the creek but the fish were all gone.

"Oh, what am I do do?" she cried. "I'm hungry and I'm miserable. If I wasn't so miserable I wouldn't be so hungry."

It was then that Catundra noticed, right in front of her nose, a pile of dirt that seemed to be moving. She watched with her head cocked to one side as that lump of dirt shrugged once and sneezed twice—revealing a small pathetic looking mole.

The mole slowly shook the dirt from his ears, rubbed the dust from his eyes and carefully looked around. "That's odd?" he said, "The sky is clear but I'm standing in a shadow. Hmmm!"

He turned around to see what was causing the shadow and sure enough there was a very hungry looking Catundra. With an "oops!" and an "Excuse me!" he made a dash back to his burrow. He had just gotten his head back into the hole, when, with one slow movement of her paw Catundra trapped that poor mole by his tail.

With a tear in her eye Catundra carefully picked up the mole and waddled back to the cabin to enjoy her melancholy meal.

"Are you going to eat me?" asked the mole.

"Yes!" sobbed Catundra.

The mole thought for a moment and then asked "Why me? I'm barely a mouthful, my fur is all full of rocks, and I probably taste like dirt. Surely there is something you would rather eat than me."

"I'm going to eat you," sobbed Catundra, "not because you are good to eat, but because there isn't anything else to eat and I have to eat because I feel so miserable."

"Now wait a minute!" said the mole indignantly, as he was dropped with a plop. "Why do you feel so miserable?"

Catundra decided to tell him the whole story of how she got just a little fat as a kitten and how all the other cats laughed and made fun of her. She went on telling how she had run away to this cabin but had no sooner arrived than all the other creatures of the forest began making fun of her too. "So, you see, little mole, the only thing that makes me happy is to eat."

It was at that moment that the mole came up with a super plan. "Cat," he said, "you're going at this all wrong. Rather than eating, you should go on a diet and get yourself in shape. If you're not fat, then nobody can make fun of you, and if they don't make fun of you, you won't be miserable and if you're not miserable you won't want to eat."

Catundra looked at the mole and thought and thought. "Maybe, little mole, you are right. But you will help me and if you are wrong I can always eat you later."

So, beginning that very day, Catundra started to exercise with the little mole. He would have her jog just a little way, then stop and let her rest. Then, when she had caught her breath and rested well, he would have her run some more, always telling her how slim and beautiful she would be.

Catundra had been exercising for days and days, and slowly but surely she was losing weight. Once in a while one of the creatures of the forest would stop and tease her, but the little mole would run them off and remind Catundra that soon they would have nothing to tease her about.

Once in a while Catundra would get that hungry look in her eye, but the little mole would wisely let her eat some fresh vegetables. Once he even let her catch a small minnow from the stream just to keep her strength.

By now Catundra had lost so much weight that the little mole had to hang on to her neck furiously as she raced about the cabin. She would run up a tree just as high and as fast as she could and then turn and dash merrily back down again. She could jump higher than she had ever been able to jump before, and you know the most surprising thing was that she wasn't sad or melancholy any more.

Most importantly, the other creatures of the forest didn't call her names because she had slimmed down to the prettiest cat they had ever seen.

And it came to be that on any beautiful summer morning you could find Catundra basking in the sunshine, with the little mole fast asleep, leaning on her knee.

SO, IF YOU'RE FAT AND
    OVERWEIGHT
AND FEELING OH SO BLUE,
REMEMBER THAT LITTLE
    RAG-TAG MOLE
AND WHAT HE HAD
    CATUNDRA DO.